The Games

By D.C. Morphis
Ellen Dee Publishing

For anyone who likes games

Chapter One

Some say it was the home run hit heard around the state, even though the sound didn't echo throughout the vast network of streets bouncing off of trees and buildings or go buzzing through everyone's brains. A bright "bang" rang strong throughout the respectable-sized stadium as a near-new wooden Louisville Slugger sharply greeted the circular object named "Rawlings." An instant smile glared from behind the new greeting as if saying, "I knew you two would get along eventually." Rawlings parted ways with his newfound friend, Louis, and began to make his acquaintance with those just beyond the fence over the left field outfielder where one unsuspecting bright-eyed youth sat eagerly at his picnic with his lucky mitt hugging the fingers of his left hand and stars in the eyes over the impending catch. The hit was almost as unexpected as the hitter. Natalie made the swing as she (yes, SHE) had done thousands of times before. Swinging the bat came easily to all the members of the Sliders; connecting their bat with the ball was an entirely different challenge. The Sliders were from Springs. They had a perfect record. Their record was so perfect they hadn't won a single game since they were added to the "circuit games" a few seasons earlier.

The Circuit was born from kids who couldn't make it on the more conventional school teams, or into any pay leagues for whatever reason. The Circuit was created on a Saturday morning, when a dutiful and doting father accepted a deeper involvement into his son's life. He watched one of his son's games and when it was over he took his son to a nearby 7-11 for a celebratory Slurpee, where he listened to him explain how the games began and why they were important. The boy's enthusiasm and passion shot quickly across the small window-side table to the loving father. Together they built the framework of the Circuit games modeling them after the knowledge they attained from watching a lifetime of professional baseball. Details were written down on nearly a dozen 7-11 napkins at first, and then transferred to the notebook that later became the Circuit handbook of instructions.

Rumors of the Circuit spread through the streets by word of mouth and text message. Team captains of no less than 10 players attended a mid-season meeting where details of the Circuit were explained. A boy named Matthew organized and presided at the meeting with his father nearby in the car waiting. The important details were typed up on two pieces of paper and handed to all captains. Team names were given to the organizer by each captain. They were written down on a notepad with the promise that the teams were or would be complete and ready by pre-season games. Individual names were not necessary since it was allowed in the handbook of instructions for a team to substitute its members as needed. No official uniforms were required according to the Circuit handbook of instructions. The only requirement for each team was to ensure the catcher had the basic protective equipment (which as defined in the handbook meant a catcher's mitt and helmet with caged front and of course an athletic cup) and for each team to provide at minimum one bat and one batting helmet. The home team was always responsible for providing an umpire, which was defined as any adult with the basic knowledge of baseball.

Matthew and his father created the framework for the Circuit games. Their involvement was quickly forgotten as the Circuit was unanimously adopted by all participants. The games became the focal point and not their origin, in fact as far as any player was concerned the games were always

there. If any player from game one in pre-season was asked how long he'd been playing in the Circuit, he'd say something like, "since I can remember." Matthew was accepted by his team members as the captain. He became the captain of the Scorpions by unanimous vote, and he took his job seriously. He took advantage of his great knowledge of every team captain and of his master list of team names by watching them all in action. He studied them, their strengths and weaknesses, in order to bring pertinent information back to his dad and the rest of the team. His dad accepted their offer as coach, a job he viewed mostly as an excuse to maintain his great relationship with his son.

The Circuit became popular. They were resigned to choose whichever field or park was available, which sometimes meant they had to use tape measures and portable bases or Frisbees or whatever they could find in order for the game to continue. Typically, they had no problem locating a simple baseball diamond at a park or school they could commandeer for one to three hours. Team captains all knew each other well since they had to keep in touch for details of upcoming games. The captains were the grapevine of the Circuit games, a sort of live network who successfully communicated any relevant information in a timely manner.

Soon after game one, the Circuit began building quite the following. There was an attraction to the games that didn't exist in quite the same manner elsewhere. The players weren't typically considered to be the most athletic, and they ranged in age from 10 to about 17. Circuit games just weren't like anything anyone had seen before, so there was an attraction or curiosity to them. Some might have said those first games were difficult to enjoy, considering the lack of coaching and perhaps skill. All would agree the players' passion for the sport was infectious. Whether the teamwork or enthusiasm for being on the field having fun was considered passion or perhaps just being part of a team, either way there was an energy that was generated that reached far beyond the playing field that attracted an audience to each game. Passion was felt each time a player swung the bat, caught a fly ball, ran the bases, or even lost a game. The sport was what was important. Their being on the field as part of something greater than oneself and the accomplishment . . . the passion for the game was converted into a power unmistakable and addictive. People who were nearby couldn't help but wonder what the commotion was about, and in so doing ended up sitting down and rooting for the weaker team.

Chapter Two

The electricity of the game stole audience members from their regularly scheduled plans onto the bleachers or at the field's edge for a baseball sojourn. This is exactly how Natalie was first introduced to the games. She was on her way to a friend's house when she unwittingly walked to the field instead. The Scorpions were playing the Wreckers at the time. This game was about mid-way through the season, so most of the players had by then landed on their feet as team-members. These teams relished in a great game of fun, battling for the win and enjoying every minute of it. The excitement grabbed Natalie and entranced her to sit down to watch. For nearly 30 minutes she forgot all about her prior engagement to look through Sophie's closet for the perfect outfit for the end of the year dance, and instead just watched the participants on the field doing a rather marvelous choreography of sporting splendor.

Natalie knew the game of baseball, but wasn't ever interested in watching before. She had more important things to do with her time, and either way, none of her friends ever seemed to be interested in sports. What she watched that day wasn't the boring brainless activity she was told about and that she avoided on the TV. She was intrigued. She was excited. She found herself cheering. She found herself asking her neighbors what the score was and who the players were. She was interested in individual players! Before she realized what was happening, her cell phone woke her up from the spell. She read her text message from Sophie that simply said, "R U coming???"

The game ended and people were getting up. She turned to leave and instead, her feet took her to the field. At first, she didn't know what she was doing by the sweaty and stinky players, but then found herself smiling and saying things like, "good game," and "that was great!"

The crowd was thinning from the bleachers and the teams were both headed to their dugouts when a boy approached her. He was no bigger than the other boys and he looked nice. His baseball cap was wet from sweat, and his blond hair stuck out the bottom on all sides but the front. She didn't have an agenda and was planning to turn to leave, but instead she stayed a moment longer to see what he would say, after all, none of the other boys took extra notice of her like this. He simply looked at her and said, "I haven't seen you here before."

As if such a simple phrase were the particular key necessary to unlock a tornado of excitement from within Natalie, she started shooting questions at him, "What is this place? What was this all about?" Natalie asked questions she didn't realize she wanted the answers for like, "Did you win?" The two of them talked for a few minutes and by the end of the conversation Matthew agreed to accept her team into the Circuit with their first game starting in two weeks. They exchanged numbers and parted smiling. Matthew needed to juggle the next two weeks' schedule in order to find a team that would play the extra game, and Natalie would need to build a team from scratch.

Natalie didn't realize just what she had done until she told Sophie the details about why she was late. Sophie reminded her that she didn't have a team and that she was crazy. "Who do you even think will play on some stupid baseball team anyway?" She was frustrated with her friend for being late and showed it with venom in her voice.

None of Sophie's negativity would ever be able to affect someone so saturated in energy and happiness. She only wished some of what had intoxicated her would spill onto her best friend in the whole world, so she could see just why she not only had to understand but had to get involved. She had to settle for old-fashioned explanation and reasoning.

"I'll just tell the guys these kids at the baseball field said they are better than us. That should get us a team of say, 10 . . . and with you, 11"

Sophie agreed her plan should work, but out rightly refused to play on any baseball team. This she insisted while looking down at her brand new matching shoes and hand bag, and holding up a colorful top Natalie hadn't ever seen before. "That's fine, you don't have to play, but at least come to the games for me." She understood her friend better than anyone in the whole world and figured at some point she would involve herself. She needed to have patience. "Ooh yea, and that top goes perfectly with those shoes!"

"I thought so too, that's why I got it out. I'll think about it- the baseball thingy," she managed to answer.

Natalie spoke with her friends one at a time and was able to put together a group of 12 who agreed to play baseball provided they have a coach, Carlos as the captain, and fancy uniforms. She agreed without hesitation knowing the fickle nature often displayed by her many friends. Since she spoke with that strange boy Matthew she knew time was a reluctant partner. She needed wings to help her catch up to the pace of the other budding and practicing teams.

The spot of captain didn't interest her anyway (she didn't really want to be any kind of a leader on an all-but-her boy's baseball team) and everyone would follow someone like Carlos, a very typical alpha male friend to all; and as for the coach, the athletic director at their school was able to refer them to someone with a coaching resume. None of them had equipment since none of them had ever played a sport in their life, and so there were a number of shopping trips in their future, something Sophie gladly agreed to manage.

Everything was moving together for her new team. She made mental check marks next to everything she thought was important for their first game that was fast approaching. She still had to let Matthew know they were ready. Her phone felt heavy, like it contained life-altering powers as she typed the simple words, "I've got my team- when & where?" She thought about whether her words were sufficiently relaying the entire message. She wondered whether he would know the text was from her. Worries quickly flew through her mind and then out of focus all-together. How many other new numbers would be texting him about having a brand new team so late in the season? . . . The meaty part of her thumb found the SEND button and pressed down. She felt the instant satisfaction of having done something good. The text was sent to Matthew and a short celebratory Mickey Mouse squeak notification tone punctuated her smile with a return text saying, "Got it! Let U know the details L8R."

"Hey Sophe, it's done. We have a baseball team!" Natalie's smile was bigger than average and Sophie could tell this meant something special to her.

"You're weird!" she replied. "Anyway, who said I was on your team? I'm not playing *baseball*." Her playful tone was evident. "Wait, does that mean we get to go shopping?!"

"Sure, I told the guys to text you their sizes, so you're good once you get those."

And that's how the Sliders were put together, though they hadn't yet earned their name. The name wasn't ever a concern of theirs. They weren't playing because any of them grew up pretending to be Babe Ruth or Jackie Robinson while swinging a stick at a rock. None of them were ever allowed to play with sticks and rocks while growing up. None of them knew what any of the professional teams were called, where any of them were, or anything about the World Series or how that worked. They thought a "foul ball" was when the ball rolled through the mud after a hit. All they knew is some other kids said they couldn't do something. They weren't going to be outdone by anyone, and since they were assured no genuine skills were required, like having to try out for a team at school, they figured they would put their money to the test and buy the skill they needed with a professional coach.

Chapter Three

Sophie had each of the team members come to her house to pick up his uniform. She was able to pass out each uniform prior to the first practice, which made the team happy since they wanted to look like baseball players to impress their new coach.

"The smelly guy at the uniform place said names go on the back with numbers. I told him he could pick the numbers and I got the names right I hope. Hope that's what you wanted,"

Sophie texted to Natalie shortly after she made the order. "And you didn't tell me what this silly team is called so I just told him we would take care of that later since the guy kind of creeped me out."

She was only able to get her new team together two times with their new coach with only a bit more than a week before their first game. Coach King used to be the head coach for some college somewhere. Natalie didn't quite retain his whole resume only that he was supposedly really good at what he did and he was old. He certainly looked the part of a coach; he was already at the field when she got there, which was about 15 minutes before the time she told everyone else. He wore a whistle around a mountain-man gray beard, sunglasses covered his sunglasses tan line, a baseball hat with probably a sports team logo sat on top of unkempt bushy hair, his physique just screamed "I used to be a great player!" with a fairly robust frame and a little gut protruding from his midsection. To top it off, he had a big odd-shaped bag with him that probably held equipment.

The rest of the team showed up right at about the time they were told, each with what looked like a brand new baseball mitt in their hands or in a shopping bag at his side. Carlos walked up to Natalie and announced he was ready to be the Captain. Everyone was lost. They were exactly where they were told to be and still were lost. Their faces showed confusion and explained they didn't know why they were there and what was expected of them.

"You're the Captain of this . . . group?" Coach King asked, butting in rather abruptly. "Then gather the guys around me now."

Carlos did what he was told, though his expression said he wasn't happy about how he was being ordered around. Everyone looked uncomfortable in their freshly starched uniforms and fashionable sneakers with their tall sports socks and mitts with purchase tags still on them.

Coach King wasn't too excited about the circumstances. He kept saying things like, "Impossible!" and, "This is ridiculous" under his breath. But when he talked to the group he always gave clear direction and tried really hard to be upbeat. When he heard when their first game was scheduled he looked away for a long minute or two and then said, "I'm going to change our strategy;" and continued with barking orders for the duration of practice.

Chapter Four

Soon after the first of the Circuit games proved successful in attracting attention and giving kids a fun time, the word spread and more teams joined. As was described in the handbook of instructions, no complete team was denied the opportunity to compete. Some teams were able to get local sponsorships from pizzerias and parent's businesses in order to acquire uniforms. The new team that had no name was different. They joined as one person and grew into a team fully backed with lots of financial means.

Natalie was seen once again by Matthew at their first game. For her team it was the first game ever played together (for most of her players, the game was the first time ever playing a sport), and for the Scorpions, the game was immediately following 20 total season games, all wins. The contrast between the two teams was drastic. Matthew didn't mean for this to happen, to showcase a team's inadequacy. With the addition of a new team introduced so late it was nearly impossible to locate a team available and willing to add an additional game to their schedule. His team was the only one willing. They were always ready for a new win. Their confidence was as solid as their team cohesion and practice vs. play rhythm. The Scorpions knew they were good and had no shame.

The Scorpions were warming up their arms in two lines spaced by about 25 feet when they saw the other team drive right up to the field in three different cars right behind their dugout. When they got out of their cars they were dressed in sharply pressed uniforms. The sight of them might have been intimidating to any on-looker with little experience with baseball. Although they looked confident enough and were well dressed they fumbled with all their gear like it was foreign to them, and they were getting dirty looks from their coach who was obviously annoyed at their ridiculous attempt at showboating.

The event was turned into a practice game in all respects if a member of the Scorpions was asked. Matthew pitched, so most of their swings would have something to find. In spite of their inability to play defense or hit the ball, and the fact their fielding was sloppier than a T-ball team, he was rather impressed with their talent for running the bases. There was more than one occasion when this team with no name was able to outrun his in-field's throws all the way to third base. If one thing was certain, this team was taught how to slide to a base, and some of them were fast.

The game ended after a quick seven innings because the Scorpions' players successfully crossed home plate 20 times compared to the team with no name's zero. According to the handbook of instructions, "if a team fails to score a single run against a team who has scored at least 15 at the close of the seventh inning, the game is over and the higher scoring team wins," otherwise, the humiliation would've been enough to convince most teams to quit the game.

After the close of the game Matthew gave Natalie a smile, a high five, and then told her he wanted to talk with her a second.

"I just wanted to let you know you guys have a name." He told her.

"Oh yeah? What name is that?" she replied.

"Well, the guys and me totally think you should call yourselves Sliders, or something like that. I mean, you guys can steal bases pretty good. I'm just saying . . . Seriously!" He continued.

"Um . . . I guess that's a compliment? . . . You guys just trashed us!"

"You'll get better. Just practice and you'll see. It was fun I hope. I mean, we had fun. I mean, it was a good game!" He finally said as he sputtered through putting his thoughts to words. As he then started to turn to give some finality to his intended brief, yet uncomfortable, conversation she broke the short silence.

"No . . . It was totally fun." She said just barely catching his attention again before he gave up on his rather pathetic attempt at being nice. "I'll let Carlos and the guys know what you said, about the name I mean."

Chapter Five

The team went back to their dugout visibly shamed. They intended on coming to the game and scoring some runs and expected to have a real chance at the baseball thing they were pushed into. They began to second-guess the reasons why they agreed to go through such torture at practice and humiliation at games. Coach King said his words of wisdom and gave them the option to stick around to work on things. The group solidly declined the offer for more torture. The coach hung around just long enough to put his things together and remind them about the next practice before walking back to the parking lot to go home.

She relayed her conversation with the captain of the Scorpions back to Carlos and a team who listened with both ears. On the one hand, they were less than thrilled about the whopping defeat, and on the other hand they couldn't deny how much fun it was applying Coach King's base stealing and simple bat swinging techniques and strategy. They couldn't debate Coach King knew a thing or two and was able to work wonders with them as a group of non-athletic individuals. They decided there was something to the "Sliders" name, and so they adopted it and immediately sent Sophie with their uniforms to get embroidered with their new team name.

When Sophie met up with the team at their next practice with the new uniforms in a box she made a confession. She admitted to watching their last game in its entirety from behind the bleachers completely out of site. "I didn't think the game was going to be so crazy exciting like it was." she acknowledged. "I was curious to see how everyone was going to do since I never saw you play before. And before I knew it I just HAD to see one of you hit the ball and then some of you DID."

Natalie knew this display all too well and decided to capitalize on it. "Does this mean you want to play on the team?" At this question moans were heard throughout the dugout as some of the newly named Sliders proudly replaced their designer polo shirts with their new uniform top. Sophie was smaller than Natalie by a few inches and never once displayed any level of athleticism in any of the years they'd known her. Yet, had she said yes they would support their friend.

"No!" She answered quick enough to put the rest of the team at ease, and with a level of disgust that rather   surprised Natalie.

"What? I thought you . . . but you were saying all those things . . . I sort of thought you wanted an invite after all that stuff you were saying . . . "she finally managed to say.

"Oh no, I can't play with you guys. I don't want to hit and catch and do all the work you guys are doing. I'm just excited to be here. Is there something else I can do besides your uniforms?"

"I guess you could just sit in the dugout with us and watch from here . . . Or maybe . . . um . . . I don't know. Guys?" Natalie was finally done thinking and decided to put the question out for the rest of the team, since after all, it was a team decision.

Coach King was beginning to get frustrated with everyone's "lollygagging" in the dugout with their friend since they were ignoring their practice hour and happened to hear enough of the conversation to help out. "If your friend wants to cheer lead for you she can get your bats and stuff at the same time." He said this to a group of baseball know-nothings and so he clarified while speaking directly to Sophie. "Little girl. Do you think you can pick up the bat after your friends hit the ball during a game?"

"Um, of course I can. Ooh, does that mean I'm on the team?!" Sophie jumped inches from the ground and clapped her hands twice. Her smile proved she was genuinely happy.

She was accepted throughout the dugout and Natalie gave her a quick hug. The coach wasted no more time, "Good, good!" and put them all to work with his improvised drills. He knew he had his work cut out for him, considering how very few could hit the ball worth a darn and their fielding skills would let his grandma get one over on them, walker and all. Even still, his base running strategy was a success. He decided to take advantage of his team's willingness to run bases and figured the hitting could come later.

The Sliders might have been a team filled entirely with bratty rich kids but the challenge of pushing themselves for the sake of the team was starting to affect them. They didn't know the difference between a double play and a single, nor were they able to differentiate between left field and right field half the time. None of them could hit the ball consistently or on purpose. Many of them still complained about their tender hands after a bad catch or from holding the bat too tight. Still, because of their miniature successes during their game with the Scorpions they were eager to learn more and keep being part of something.

Their strategy was to get on base however they could (occasionally with a solid base hit), and then to steal their way home sliding into one base at a time. This carried them through the season as they stole base after base. Their season ended with the only undiscovered base being the home plate.

Coach King suggested they practice off-season, but the team said "no". Carlos stated, "we are improving and it's still fun, so we'll see you next season. I'll make sure to keep in touch." The rest of the team, except for Natalie agreed. They had been getting more beat up then they ever thought possible between the games and Coach King's practices.

None of them were accustomed to the 'hard labor'. But Natalie wanted more, although she didn't dare mention what exactly she wanted to the rest of the team or even Coach King. She didn't even know what she wanted exactly. She wanted more baseball. She wanted to get better. She wanted more fun.

Natalie was an average player on the Sliders. In fact, she was marginal at best. She wasn't the fastest, strongest, or smartest. She was the only girl, and because she was the only girl she was probably the hardest worker out of them all. She struggled for acceptance from the rest of the team. Her second base position, though not always the most demanding, was still trying her. Her fielding was only showing moderate improvement, and her batting was atrocious. The bat never felt at home in her hands. She didn't feel confident anywhere else but while running from base to base, and that wasn't good enough for her.

She confided in Sophie that she wanted to keep practicing once a week but didn't know how to do this all by herself. In the back of her mind, she wondered what telling Sophie was going to do.

The reason she was confiding was purely because she needed some support and a best friend was readily available.

Sophie listened intently to everything her friend was confessing and then an amazing thing happened. She came up with a solution that might work.

"How about going to those places at family fun parks with the fenced areas for hitting the ball? At least I think that's what people do in those things . . . Wouldn't those help you practice?" She had a look on her face that suggested the gears were turning and she was in genuine help mode.

"Sure . . . you're talking about the batting cages. I thought of that, but I need to practice my catching too . . ." Natalie was concerned with finding a willing subject to help her with her catching. She thought of asking her parents to help, but her dad could only possibly help every once and a while, maybe every other two weeks or so when he became available from work, and her mom was more like Sophie, willing to cheer and be involved, but not in the physical way.

"But, do you have to only HIT the ball when you're in there? Couldn't you be in there with your glove instead of the bat and practice catching AND throwing . . . ?" Sophie still tried her best to help her friend in her moment of brainstorming.

"That's a great idea!" Natalie was so clearly excited about the idea of a weekly training in the batting cages she didn't even let her friend finish the thought. There was no reason she could think of that would prevent her from going in the cage with just her glove.

The off season was spent as usual, with school and some extra-curricular shopping to keep Sophie happy, and then also in the batting cages once a week for at least a straight hour each time. She worked herself so hard that it didn't take long for some of her Sliders friends to notice what she was doing.

◆

One day, while Matthew was at the family fun center to play miniature golf with his mom, dad, and little sister Eloise, he noticed Natalie in the cages. Every time he came to the center he would look to see what sort of competition was swinging the bat. This time the competition was a familiar face. The strange thing was she didn't have a bat in her hand, but a glove. She had the setting on what looked like the slow pitch baseball and she was catching the ball as though she was in a game, and then she placed the ball to the side. He then watched her pick up those placed balls and toss them to herself to hit the way a coach might to give his infield some fielding practice. He pointed her out to his dad who had been watching about as much as him and simply said, "Huh, that's a good idea."

She was different. He normally had little respect for the rich kids he knew. She was different. He hadn't ever seen anyone use the cages this way before. Whenever he wanted to throw the ball around he always either asked his dad or met up with a friend. This display explained more about her than he knew. She was different. She should be recognized.

Chapter Six

Two additional seasons passed in much the same way as the first. A few more teams were added each season as word spread and popularity grew. The Scorpions were rarely challenged at first place and they remained undefeated. Matthew continued his job as Captain of his team as his own father coached them to victory upon victory. The end of the third season was fast approaching and as he looked at the game schedule he put together he noticed they were slotted to play against the Sliders. This would be their first game since the only game together the year previous. He worried. What worried him wasn't that he thought a team tied for last place ever stood a chance at beating the number one team, but because he understood the Sliders possibly better than any other team in the Circuit. His own team didn't have the slightest idea, and he didn't feel they were prepared.

The Sliders were the biggest joke the Circuit games had ever known when they first started. Two and a half years later and teams still use the game of the Scorpions and Sliders (although they were still un-named for that game) as a low score indicator. If a team lost by more than 15 points they were publicly compared with the Sliders until they played their next game. They were called Nothings in memory of and to mock the only team in Circuit history who played a game without a name.

The general opinion of the Sliders wasn't accurate. Matthew had briefed his coach more than once about the dangers of their improvement and Natalie's growing determination. He explained to his dad how he witnessed the Sliders' coach move her from second base to short stop during one of their games. He explained how her hits were getting more consistent and it looked like she was correctly predicting ball placement as it crossed the plate. He explained how the entire team had improved in hitting and running bases, though he admitted they still failed to score runs. He had long fruitless discussions with his coach dad over the season's team details from time to time. He said the same thing almost with each discussion. "I understand your concerns . . . You know you're doing a great job scouting the competition. Don't worry, we'll be ready."

That was the end of it every time. Since even Matthew wasn't certain there was need to worry about a game with such a low ranking team he let it drop. He saw that Natalie had more heart than anyone else on her team, and in fact she had more heart than most people on all the other teams too. He understood that with their paid coach and fancy equipment it was only a matter of time before they won their first game. Part of him wanted to lose to the Sliders so everyone would see he wasn't crazy. Part of him wanted them to win knowing it would be Natalie who was going to bring them down.

Several wins later and the Scorpions vs. Sliders was reality. He could tell his teammates and coach were still unprepared. They didn't even consider them challengers and said things like, "let's have a good practice out there," and, "try not to hit too many home runs this time," or, "Just don't get hurt out there."

Carlos met Matthew at home plate to shake hands. They both appeared confident as they each wished the other a good game. The Sliders started in the outfield and everything began.

Both teams were strong, and seemed to thirst after a win. Already, the Scorpions recognized this wasn't the same team they played two years ago. This wasn't even the same team they played the year before. They had a hunger about them. Perhaps they were finally tired of being last place. Perhaps they received a "pep" talk from the re-incarnated Willy Mays or baseball's great Ken Griffey Jr. Whatever they did seemed to be working. The Scorpions struggled to get on base, and when they did they were thrown out first chance Sliders got.

"What's gotten into you boys?" His dad's voice hit a nerve. His voice was seldom heard during game time. He did his training at practices and left game day up to the others with very little intervention. He believed in letting them work out their problems on their own, and typically only piped up to give positive reinforcement. "You aren't playing like yourselves today!" His words weren't coming out as hurtful attacks, but rather confused.

The whole team shared a silence that spoke louder than words.

Jimmy the catcher finally made eye contact with the coach, which was something everyone else had been purposely avoiding and simply lied. "Just want them to feel good before we really hit em hard is all." Even as he spoke, the grunts told the truth. The Scorpions were dumbfounded. They weren't playing terribly, and yet they weren't scoring runs against the worst rated team in the entire league. The coach wasn't pleased with the response and yet sat down and accepted it, just as these boys accepted the Sliders. Their performance was self-defeating and short of an attitude adjustment, the game wasn't going to improve.

One inning concluded as the next began with the same results. Each team produced zero input for the scoreboard. The side of the Scorpions seethed with frustration while the side of the Sliders bubbled in excitement and encouragement. The stands, mostly eager Circuit fans impatient to witness another Scorpions slaughter were instead on the edge of their seats and on and off their

phones sharing updates with the other Circuit teams.

Matthew was pitching his heart out for the Scorpions. One strike after another became his pattern up until the 6th Inning when the Slider's began making solid and regular contact with the ball. Infield and outfield ensured none of those hits bore any fruit. Yet another inning closed and the Sliders were stopped. The latest series of hits scared Matthew for what might be coming. He knew his arm was getting tired and he could see their hitting greatly improved.

Scorpions made good use of their bats at the end of the 6th with one run batted in. As Carlos pitched his best version of a change-up (possibly his finest pitch), his opponent found and destroyed the ball, and then discovered third base. An inside fast ball was sent right down the third base line to bring the Scorpions a highly desired run placing the batter at first base with only one out. Carlos then made good use of his mitt as he caught a surprising line drive hit that nearly drove his head to the parking lot. As soon as he realized what he managed to do he contacted first base and accomplished their first double play to end the 6th inning. The base runner at 1st never thought in a million years a line drive like that could've been stopped by a member of the Sliders.

Only Matthew really understood what was happening. He knew the Sliders were going to be a team hungry for approval. The team didn't take the Sliders seriously ever since their first game together ended in a 20-0 massacre. Was this going to be a learning lesson on humility?

Starting in the 7th inning, faces of defeat and perplexity worn by the Scorpions spawned a sloppiness that couldn't be controlled. Fly balls disappeared into the clouds or by sunlight, and a couple times the outfield over-threw their cutoff man. Their at bat resulted in strikeouts and foul balls or overrun bases that ended in outs. They managed to take the Sliders to the 9th inning holding desperately to their one run earned early in the sixth. They knew if they could just stop them at the bottom of the 9th, they would walk away with the win.

The Scorpions were blinded by confusion at the Sliders' unexperienced successes. Matthew's pitches were strong and yet three Sliders' batters were able to connect with the ball and take their base making it three's a crowd in the Scorpions' infield. There was one out remaining before the

Scorpions could finally claim the pathetic win of one run. The pressure had been on Matthew to finish the game strong with the remaining few pitches instead of handing the ball to their one available relief pitcher.

Natalie had been swinging two bats in order to warm up her arms while waiting her turn. She carefully handed one of her bats to her best friend Sophie and stepped up to the plate. "Hey Nat, you GOT this!" Sophie's voice sounded tough over all other ambient noises. No other sound broke her concentration as she stood beside home plate. She was all alone with the boy she'd seen time and time again at her games and the family fun center. She felt oddly comfortable swinging at his pitches. She successfully hit a single and a double before this at bat. Typically she wasn't considered a big concern for hitting strong enough to do the ultimate damage since she was a girl. Most people in the stands would've predicted she be the end of the Scorpions' torture session. Matthew intended to get her to pop the ball up for an easy out, or to simply get her to swing and miss those high fastballs. He remembered learning that the high fastball is her most difficult pitch.

Signs were given to Jimmy, who then relayed them to Matthew. The first pitch suggestion was a

fastball low and outside. Matthew shook his head.
Another sign was then relayed to throw high and
inside. With the nod of his head he prepped
himself for his first pitch. The ball was thrown with
a grunt that told all within ear shot this was a fast
pitch. The ball was thrown too far inside to be
considered a strike and was rightfully left a "ball"
by Natalie. Matthew's arm was tired. He knew his
dad wanted him to finish the game with the last
few pitches, and so he tried his best to wear
confidence. He was on reserve energy, and Jimmy
knew it. His first pitch to Natalie let Jimmy know
the fastball might not be fast or high.

The next pitch was called to go high and to
the outside. That pitch was intended to confuse
the batter into letting a perfectly good strike pass
right by unknowingly. Matthew rotated the ball in
his hand over and over as he nervously aligned the
laces just right under his fingers. He looked
intently at Natalie who stared right back at him.
She didn't seem the least bit nervous. Under the
circumstances, many players would feel the weight
of all the well wishers and crack under pressure by
over reaching for the big hit and instead popping
the ball just overhead.

He loosened his grip as though he'd been
squeezing an orange and not a laced up ball of

smooth leather around tightly wound string, tensed his arm, and flailed it out from the side as a catapult might throw a giant boulder to break down a defensive wall of a castle. He couldn't help the expression on his face at the release of the ball from his hand. The ball left his hand too early. The early release placed the ball at the desired height, but the spin on the ball carried it to the right, placing it over the plate as a high center fast ball rather than going high and to the outside.

Natalie saw the pitch release and was ready. The ball was coming towards her exactly how she liked them, high and centered. She trained for this very moment, and she knew what she had to do. The ball slowed to a near stop as she became mentally equipped for the precise moment. She stepped about six inches to the left with her lead foot, tightened her left hand grip as she commanded cooperation from her bat, and swung at that high fast ball just as the ball reached the front of the plate. She timed her swing so the ball would be sent safely to the right of the third base line soaring over the third baseman and shortstop into left field.

She looked closely at the ball as it came within her reach. Time stood still for her. If she wanted, she could have put down her bat, run around the bases, and then run around the pitcher's mound making silly faces at the pitcher before returning to swing at the same ball. She memorized the ball. There were scuffmarks just above one of the laces from when the ball either hit the dirt or made contact with bat. The title "Rawlings" spun over and over as the ball invited her to give it another purpose. It taunted the very baseball bat she held in her hand.

"I dare you to hit me. I double dog dare you to even try!" The ball taunted the ready Louisville Slugger until it couldn't handle anymore mocking, and that's when it happened. A bright "Bang" rang strong throughout the respectable-sized stadium as a near-new wooden Louisville Slugger sharply greeted the circular object named "Rawlings." The instant smile from behind the proud owner of such a brave bat watched with glee as Rawlings parted ways with his new found friend, Louis, and began to make his acquaintance with those just beyond the fence over left field where one unsuspecting bright-eyed youth opened his mitt as the stars in his eyes quickly turned into a fast-approaching baseball.

She swung with all her might; a strength that was charmed by an impending win. She swung with all her heart; just before her chest burst from within. She swung for all the girls in the stands who anxiously awaited the outcome, and who longed for her success. She swung for all those naysayers who didn't believe she was capable. She swung for her friend Sophie. Lastly, she swung for the love of the game.

Just as Matthew let go of the ball he knew there was danger. He knew she was capable of making contact, but never would've guessed she was able to do so much damage with the one hit.

The ball screamed over third base with a strong steady stride. With two outs the base runners didn't bother to wait until the ball was confirmed safe. They put their speed to the test to discover their home for the first time against the Scorpions, against anyone. It wasn't until Natalie had reached first base that the Scorpions realized what just happened. But Natalie knew as soon as her bat made contact with the ball, in fact as soon as she woke up that morning she knew this would happen.

She accomplished the unthinkable. She hit the grand slam home run that shattered both team's perfect records. Legend of her hit raced through the streets from team to team across the whole state in a matter of minutes as cell phone after cell phone lit up with text messages and video. Sophie had been video recording the whole at bat. She knew the capabilities of her best friend. Well, she might not have known like Natalie knew, but she hoped. Natalie's name became respected as a real ball player on par with even the best of the Circuit players.

Instead of winning the game with a few pitches, Matthew ended the game with the most incredible display he'd seen in his whole life. He watched Natalie round the bases and instead of being angry, he found himself smiling. He took his glove off his hand and held it down at his side in utter defeat. His team was caught off guard. Some of them stood still at their positions watching the end unfold before them. The others began a casual jog back to their dugout for the traditional celebratory post game high-fives and accolades; only this time there was silence.

The Sliders welcomed their new star at home plate and lifted her into the air like they just won the World Series game. The chants and cheers from the bleachers lured people from the streets onto the field. The excitement at that game was unmatched. Even the Scorpions couldn't resist the excitement forever. They lined up to shake hands and give their congratulations. After all, they were a reasonable team with a true love of the game. Although they were humbled, they would look back on the day's events with a fonder respect for the Sliders and baseball, knowing that anyone with the right determination and passion can play and succeed.

Carlos later nominated Natalie as their Team Captain. Her hard work ethics were adopted by the rest of the team. To Coach King's surprise, she had everyone coming to the field one hour before the start of their games to discuss strategies and work on drills in addition to their weekly practices. The Sliders started to win more of their games. Their reputation followed them everywhere they played. Natalie was faced with the almost weekly decision to turn down other teams' scouting offers. The Sliders were rarely under estimated after that game; in fact many of the Sliders officially decided to audition for college baseball when the time came. Natalie's grand slam hit affected every team within the Circuit. One might have said her single hit changed the way he viewed the game.

Images of an elated Natalie rounding the bases, and the ready embraces from the rest of the

Sliders who gathered at home plate, were swiftly uploaded onto Youtube and the Circuit's Facebook page. Several pictures of the Scorpions' defeated faces were also quickly advertised in various places on the World Wide Web. One picture, fit for the cover of TIME magazine caught a catcher just after removing a sweat-filled mask from his face.

The Sliders began as individuals who valued material possessions and popularity among life's most important goals. They discovered greater treasures existed. They discovered that cheers for a good catch or a good hit far outweighed the compliments given for apparel. Hard work was no longer shrugged off as something for the less accomplished and privileged. The games changed them. They had more purpose because of the games.

The teamwork and enthusiasm for being on the field as part of a team generated an energy that reached far beyond the playing field. Passion was felt each time they swung the bat, caught a fly ball, ran the bases, or even lost a game. That passion transferred into their daily living. The sport proved to be more important than they could've possibly guessed. Being a part of something greater held significant meaning. The game stole each member of the Sliders from his regularly scheduled plans onto the field for a baseball sojourn that changed his life.

Epilogue

Having just finished such a monumental life achievement, The Sliders were left with stories, pictures, and first-account memories. They attended their classes learning about the American Revolution, solving quadratic equations, and debating about whether Fahrenheit 451 was meant to be literal or figurative. What they wanted was a Circuit Games sequel.

At lunch that same day, many of them sat around their table outside just like usual until Jimmy spoke up.

"So, we had this poetry assignment in English class a few days ago . . ."

The assignment was to write poetry that was centered on the student's passions. In Jimmy's class the teacher gave an example of Henry (he really goes by "Hank"), a boy who is known for playing guitar and who also sat in the second row sometimes WITH his guitar. He could write poems about playing, music in general, or even just about the guitar as a physical instrument, like how it feels to hold and what it's like using a guitar pick. He then went on a long discussion about how poems have been turned into songs for centuries.

All that was great, but soon the teacher gave his second example of Ron and his love of basketball. Ron was on the school Varsity Basketball team, and everyone knew he was good. Well, the teacher went on and on about how poems could be written about anything and everything, "even playing a sport," he said. Jimmy's mind was awoken to activity. He almost immediately pulled out a pad of paper from his bag and started writing bits and pieces of poems based on the many poems they had been studying for the previous few days.

His obvious discomfort at bringing up such a taboo subject among friends was nearly enough to silence the bunch, if they hadn't all been thinking the same exact thing.

"Yeah, I think we had the same assignment, and I gotta tell you, that was pretty cool." Carlos continued, a little less uncomfortably than did Jimmy. "I thought it'd be stupid when he first talked about how we need to write about something we're passionate about, but then I couldn't stop thinking about popping one over left field and I guess my first poem just wrote itself."

"Or watching the face on that Matthew kid from the Scorpions go white as a ghost as I go casually round third." interrupted Natalie. "Wait, just how many poems DID you write?" But Carlos conveniently ignored her question, or was just too slow as others began sharing their own flood of memories.

"He became a Casper copy alright!" Sophie contributed, with a bout of hearty laughter.

Gaining courage, Jimmy decided to let his apprehension loose from its batter's cage.

"So you guys have been writing about the Games too?"

"Yeah!" Their discovery didn't come as much of a shock to any of them as they looked around the table at each other's growing smiles.

"Well," he continued, "I can't tell you how much fun I've been having with this assignment. Ooh, check out this one." His hand went into his bag to search for a notepad so he could look through his bits and pieces of possible poems to find his choicest finished few.

They spent the remainder of lunch sharing their creations with each other. Their words flowed through their pens and onto notepads as they relived their emotions. They shared their excitement for hitting the ball, catching a "pop fly", or running around the bases. The sorrows of defeat were delicately defined and beautifully delivered on paper. The thrill of the win was remarkably reborn in ink.

It took no time at all for each teacher to see the changes in not only the few outwardly excited students, but in the others as well.

Many shared their love for the game the best they could in poetry as rumor traveled around the campus that writing was now socially accepted. The halls were decorated in the student's more notable works. Instead of students getting in trouble for passing notes in class, they would get in trouble for passing poems.

As for the Sliders, they were happy regardless what the rest of student body chose to do with their time. They continued to practice during their off time (have to keep those Scorpions under control after all) and as long as they had a pad and a pen they were always kept busy working on some choice rhyming for the next batch of works to share at lunch with pals.

ODE to Scorpions

By Carlos

You think you're so good
You think you're all that
You think that you could
Destroy us with that bat!

I have news for you today!
This victory might have been yours
But it might be too soon to shout Hooray
Because this defeat only opened doors.

We will soon uncover hidden talents
You will soon see
So get out the s'mores and pitch your tents
We'll even have to charge a fee.

The crowds are sure to come
Whether a practice or a game
We're coming out to get some
And we won't be tame.

Your turn will come soon enough
To check on our progress first hand.
Don't hold back, be sure to be tough
The show will be amazing for those in the stand.

We'll make you think you're ahead
Make you think you're still better
We'll soon gain strength instead
And watch closely as you fetter.

You will start making dumb mistakes
You will begin dropping balls
We will no longer be seen as rich flakes
We will refuse to take more falls!

I foresee the day we beat you
That day your sand castle crumbled
That day we'll be a team brand new
And the mighty Scorpions humbled.

Gave his Life
By Jimmy

I'm grateful to the pig or cow
Who made it possible for me now
To catch a ball moving at great speeds
A protection that prevents palm bleeds

Practice
By Natalie

It starts with a run
And continues in fun
As long as you like pain
Or playing in the rain.

How many times must I catch a ball?
Or learn how to take a fall?
How many laps will it take?
To leave our opponents in our wake?

Whether I am swinging a bat
Or reaching first base in four flat
I know after a day's gruel
And feeling like the team's Mule.

I am way more equipped
After having been coach-whipped
Than just walking off the street
As baseball fresh meat.

Wonder Bat
By Natalie

My bat is wonderful
And it's full of wood.
It's not that it's colorful
If only everyone just understood!

This bat gave me my first
My first real hit.
It gave me the thirst
One unquenchable by any fancy mitt.

I swung my bat with ease
At every good-looking pitch.
And when that bat connected
I'd almost go weak in the knees.

The joy is unmeasurable
To feel my bat send a ball packing.
A feeling nearly unattainable
Punctuated by a sharp snapping.

For one to understand
He must give it a try.
I can't promise bliss for every eager hand,
To know what I mean, just make the ball fly!

The Catch
By Jimmy

To send the ball packing
With my hardest whacking
Out to the stands
To so many eager open hands.

I long to be the one
The audience talks about.
To provide the ball of fun
That feels so sturdy and stout

That inflicts a welcoming sting
To the palm of a protected hand
After the metallic "pling"
Resounding from the depths of the batter's sand

And to watch the rehearsed cheer
With arms extended
And the inevitable tear
And chorus blended.

One stands in his young age
As he celebrates
His victorious package
Wrapped in leathery restraints.

Leathery Palm
By Stuart

Oh, to wear the glove all the time
To have it with me always.
I could practice all days
In the grocery store with a . . . lime.

My skills would triple what they were
As my hand began growing fir.
That fir would get thicker
And nearly stop my mom's . . . ticker

But worry not, I'd tell her
The hand is only preparing
For all the practicing in winter
My hand is planning on fairing.

I plan to become real great
At this game I love so dearly!
For next season I can't hardly wait
I can see it so clearly.

It will take all my efforts
And a hand that's really tough.
I'll practice with things of all sorts
Nothing will seem to be enough.

Pressure
By Scott

The team feels heaving on my back,
Won't someone take up some slack?
I know everyone wants the same,
To win each and every game.

But sometimes I feel
As though I need to kneel
To find strength and help
Rather than look to my team 'n yelp.

The burden of success is great,
Possibly too much for my young state.
And might be better shared
By a team with players who cared.

What should I do, who can I call?
Before this stress causes me to fall?
I'd like to have someone to hail
So when the time comes I don't fail.

Coaches Magic Glasses
By Natalie

Had I magic glasses, ones that could see
My sliders victorious in front of me.
With magic glasses upon my face,
My team all keeping up the pace,

At their positions on hand with glove,
Overhead, some cooing of the field dove.
As I look through these glasses of mine,
holding that maple, a stick so fine

The thunder stick firmly in hand
A swift swing sends a ball out of this land
My magic glasses would capture all
Every freckle, every hair, every tumble, every fall.

One thing my glasses do not need to see,
The smile on mom 'n dad's faces and their cheerful
glee.
A delight that derives from these parents' offspring
And what their future and success will bring

Of such, even a coach is made proud
Joy, admiration, a feeling so loud
Emotions that come straight from the heart
Because of players doing more than their part

Homework
By Sophie

As if school work wasn't enough
And practices not already tough.
In order to ensure my team's success
I research the other team's strengths and stuff.

This self-inflicted chore
Is one I alone have bore
To see my team's cheer, no less
Is excitement I could never ignore.

My team's success I share
I think it only fair
If I were to guess
Efforts are acknowledged – that they care.

Of course it's not me alone
Sitting upon some kind of throne
Using magical sort of finesse
One from Merlin, but on loan.

My part I feel is valuable,
A sort I cannot label
But am glad my coach does bless
And will forever contribute as long as able.

Tough
By Anonymous

I want to be tough,
I want to be strong,
I want to belong,
And that needs to be enough!

Little Do They Know
By Jimmy

The pitcher throws the ball
But little do they know
The ball could go fast
Or the ball could go slow.

The magic is knowing
Before all the throwing,
Who the batter is, his strengths,
Before his bat reaches those lengths.

Little do they know
The pitcher does throw the ball
But they think I only crouch low
And catch the ball so it wont fall

I have a secret to tell.
The pitcher doesn't know each batter that well.
I too do homework; info I do not sell.
But don't worry, I won't let my ego swell.

Water
By Tommy

No drink is more satisfying
On or off the field
Than the one I bring
And intend without yield

To consume after exertion
The liquid so clear
That contributed to my creation
And lubricated my every gear

My Big Patch of Grass
By Alexander

Why would I want a single base
When I have this spacious place?
What's so special about the infield?
Standing upon his white shield . . .

Mine isn't an area small
And is hardly shared.
After the ball is hit and begins to fall
And passes over standing players paired,

The job becomes mine alone
To follow the ball and judge,
(A skill that took a while to hone)
And cannot by one easily fudge.

I must ready and steady my glove
As my feet transport me to the right spot.
The process takes real love,
Something it's easy to see I've got.

The end result is clear to me,
Any novice can clearly see.
Though others might get more glory,
Now you can see there's another story.

Never Knew
By Natalie

My dad always works
He hardly ever plays.
He's sometimes gone for days,
Something he says really pays.

He doesn't have any hobbies,
Just surfs the net and stuff.
I don't really see him enough,
With me, he says he doesn't want to be too tough.

About half-way into the season
He said one day he'll stay home,
And at my game he may roam,
That I will be his reason.

Perhaps online he'd now seen it all
So now there's time to watch me hit a ball,
Either way it's entirely his call
To finally spend some time with me.

He said it's my turn and work can wait,
That he doesn't mind being late.
With me he wants a clean slate,
A chance to get to know me.

He's become my biggest fan
And comes to every game he can.
I'm finally part of his plan!
It's good to know he truly loves me.

Soaring
By Sebastian

Where only birds fly
And maybe airplanes.
As the trees pass them by
And their speed gains.

Long for the view
And to watch the sky blue
To see the clouds all fluffy
Up where it can't ever feel stuffy.

My goal is so simple,
To soar high over the furthest wall,
To stay within each side's pole
Before deciding to fall.

The Greatest Game
By Collin

Have you some peanuts
Have you some cracker jacks
Sit down, enjoy
Put down that electronic toy!

From the first pitch to the last
This game will be a blast
Whether cheering for a mate
Or eating hotdogs on a plate,

You'll be on the edge of your seat
Tapping your foot to a subtle beat
Soaking in all the sights and sounds
Eating popcorn by the pounds.

As the bat connects with a thunderous crack
It matters very little what team you back
Because the love of the game drew you near
As you let that passion control and steer

The greatest game cannot disappoint;
It cannot let you down.
Snug that glove tight on that hand
And ready the nest for the determined ball to land.

The Devil Inside
By Andrew

He told me baseball sucks
He told me not to try
He fed me lots of excuses
He even taught me to lie.

He wanted me to fail
He wanted my team to fail
And took glory as losses continued to climb.
He helped me to waste my time . . .

I'll show that stupid devil!
Show him my drive isn't just level.
He'll see me AND my effort
Every time my cleats touch dirt.

He can't ignore my positive morale,
Stuff admired by even my worst pal.
My smile will sting him, it's simple,
Punctuated every time with either dimple.

That dumb devil will really see
His words and ideas can never bend.
His power cannot affect me
My potential is limitless and cannot end.
So BACK OFF!

The Buzz
By Arnold

The static sounds grow louder
With every moment exciting.
Cheers, clapping, and clamor
And all their happiness do sing.

The cheers bring courage
And the courage performance.
Fun and happiness nourish,
The buzz, which quickly enhance.

The Adversary
By Steve

Often one step ahead
And sometimes hard to see.
Able to fly high in the sky
Higher than the tallest tree.
Difficult to hit
And sometimes hard to catch
If you know what I mean . . .

Tricky, Tricky, Tricky
By Shawn

Straight down the center!
This time it will be hit,
It will be hit hard!
It doesn't stand a chance
And will not escape!
It's sender stares earnestly
But will not be satisfied!
I ready my hands,
And strengthen my grip
Advance my lead foot for power
And swinggg . . . NNOOOO!
What happened? It changed direction!
How could I have? . . .
How could it be so? . . .
What was . . . um . . .
That's just not . . .!
Oh, I'll be sure to get the next one.

Sky High
By Eloise

Oh, if I could fly,
If I could fly sky high
If I could soar
If I could soar way off the dirt floor
Then I might see
A cheering crowd looking for me
With a background so blue
Oh let it be true
No person can frown
As my laces touch down
And the rolling comes to a stop
Without so much as a hop
That my flight was not in vain
And my team's score not remain
But instead, follow my path,
And exercise in math
To defy physic's law
A never come down flaw
Which makes them the victors
And puts them in pictures
And raises their spirits sky-high

She Came!
By Natalie

The sky's blue had gotten grayer
The air started feeling yucky.
The team was un-playable, just ask any league
player
The over all mood was mucky

Each time at bat
Was losing it's excitement
Even the feel of my hat
Was more like parchment.

Then the familiar voice called my name
It took but a moment for me to see
Her standing and verbally giving me fame
Is that something I could be?

A smile stole my face.
And Hector stole his second base
It was my turn to take the bat
All the sudden the air no longer felt flat

I had a fan all to me
Who knew just what I could be
I'm so glad she came
This game will definitely not be the same

www.ingramcontent.com/pod-product-compliance
Lightning Source LLC
Chambersburg PA
CBHW070535130626
46555CB00003B/1435